CLASSIC COLLECTION

THE ADVENTURES OF
TOM SAWYER

MARK TWAIN

ADAPTED BY SAVIOUR PIROTTA · ILLUSTRATED BY ALFREDO BELLI

NEW
BURLINGTON
BOOKS

Tom Learns a Valuable Lesson

"Tom Sawyer, where do you think you're going?"

"Swimming in the river, Aunt Polly."

Aunt Polly stood blocking the doorway, a paintbrush in her hand.

"I told you that because you had been fighting on Thursday, I'd have a job for you on Saturday."

Tom groaned. Aunt Polly was good to him and his brother Sid. She'd taken them in when their own mother had passed away, even though she had her own daughter, Mary, to look after. But, sometimes, she could be so hard on them.

"Paint the garden fence with whitewash, Tom," she said. "All thirty feet of it." She led Tom outside, where a large bucket of whitewash stood by the fence.

"You start painting, Tom," she warned, "and don't come back in until you've done the whole fence."

Tom started painting, wondering how on earth he was going to finish the job without both arms falling off. It was a lovely day too. Tom reckoned every other boy in his town of St Petersburg was going down to the river.

His friend Ben Rogers came strolling down the street, munching on an apple.

"Say, Sawyer, you ain't going swimming today? I guess you have work to do, huh?"

"This ain't work," said Tom. "It's only work when you have to do something you don't want to do."

"You mean you *want* to be whitewashing that fence?" gawped Ben.

"Does a boy get to whitewash a fence every day?" said Tom, painting the wooden fence with enthusiasm.

"I guess not," replied Ben. "I say, Tom, will you let me paint a little?"

"I can't," said Tom. "Aunt Polly's awful particular about her fence. Got to be done right."

"I'll give you the core from my apple," promised Ben.

"Nope."

"I'll give you the whole apple."

Tom handed over the paintbrush, pretending to be worried about letting Ben do some whitewashing. Inside, though, he was grinning like a cat. He'd found a way to avoid doing any work.

Ben started whitewashing. Tom sat in the shade, munching on the apple. Soon other friends came by. They all wanted to have a go with the paintbrush. Tom got them all to pay something and by the time the whitewash ran out, he'd earned a collection of small toys and fruit. And the fence had three coats of whitewash!

Tom smiled to himself. He'd learned a valuable lesson that morning. If you want to make people really want something, you have to make it hard to get.

Aunt Polly came out and nearly fainted with surprise when she found the whole job done!

"Well, I never, Tom" she gasped. "I think you deserve an ice cream."

A Hard Girl to Get

There was a big pile of furniture outside Judge Thatcher's house. Someone was moving in with Judge Thatcher, who'd come to live next door to Aunt Polly a year ago. Tom was passing and stopped to look.

The newcomer was in the garden. She was about Tom's age, with yellow pigtails and a summer frock.

Tom's heart skipped a beat. What a beautiful girl! An angel! Tom started doing cartwheels across the street, hoping to get her attention. The girl ignored him and picked flowers. By late afternoon, all the girl's belongings had been moved indoors. She disappeared inside too, throwing a squashed pansy over the fence.

Tom pounced on the flower. He had to speak to that girl, tell her… how much he wanted to be with her.

When Aunt Polly had gone to bed, he sneaked out and slipped over the fence to Judge Thatcher's house. There was a light on in one of the upstairs windows. He could see the girl's shadow moving across the curtain. He hoped she would come to the window and talk to him, but she put out the light. Suddenly Tom felt very sad. If he couldn't spend the rest of his life with that girl, he didn't want to live at all.

Tom heard an upstairs window open. A moment later he was drenched in cold water.

"Go away, you rascal," said a grown-up voice, "or next time I'll empty the chamber pot on you."

Tom leaped to his feet and jumped back over the fence. That girl was sure going to be hard to get.

Tom got to school late on Monday morning.

"Mr Sawyer," thundered the schoolmaster. "What time do you call this?"

"Sorry sir," replied Tom. "I bumped into Huckleberry Finn."

Everyone gasped. Huckleberry Finn was a homeless scamp. He never went to school or church. All the children had been told not to talk to him.

"Take off your jacket," hissed the teacher. When Tom had done so, he gave Tom a beating with his cane for being late and for talking to Huckleberry Finn.

"Sit with the girls," he said when he had finished.

There was only one empty seat with the girls. And it was right next to the new girl. Tom couldn't believe his luck. "I seen you at Judge Thatcher's house," he whispered. "Are you a relative of his?"

"He's my father. Mum and I were staying with an aunt till the house was ready."

"What's your name?" asked Tom.

"Becky. What's yours?"

"Tom Sawyer."

While the schoolmaster's back was turned, Tom placed a peach on Becky's desk. "Please take it," he scrawled on his writing slate. "I've got plenty more."

He rubbed that message out and started drawing.

"What are you drawing, Tom? Let me see."

Becky pushed away his arm. "Why, it's a house. You're a good artist, Tom. Can you draw me?"

Tom did. Then he scribbled something.

"What's that you're writing, Tom?" Becky pushed his hand away gently. I LOVE YOU, it read.

"Why, Tom, that's a bad thing to write."

But Tom could tell by her smile that she was pleased.

The lunchtime bell rang. "Sit by me in the playground. I'll teach you to draw," said Tom

"Okay," said Becky. They sat on the wall, drawing.

"Tell me you love me," said Tom, "and then we'll be engaged."

"Okay. I love you, Tom," whispered Becky.

"I love you," replied Tom.

"It feels great being engaged," sighed Becky. "Will we walk to school together every day?"

"Of course," said Tom. "When I was engaged to Amy Lawrence…"

Tom realized that he'd made a big mistake. Tears welled up in Becky's eyes. "You've been engaged before!"

"I don't care for anyone but you, Becky," said Tom. He fished in his pocket for his favourite thing, a large brass doorknob. "Take this, Becky."

She slapped his hand and his treasure rolled across the ground. Tom stared at it, feeling very upset. Then he bolted.

"Tom, come back," called Becky.

But Tom was already up the road.

Murder in the Graveyard

"Hello Tom," said Huckleberry Finn. "You running away from school?"

"I'm never going back," replied Tom. He'd bumped into Huckleberry Finn again on Collier Hill. "Why have you got a dead cat, Huck?"

"It's to remove a wart on my hand," said Huck. "Don't you know dead cats are good for removing warts? You have to stand over a wicked person's grave with a cat in your left hand. At midnight, devils will come to fetch the wicked person to hell. You throw the dead cat after them and the wart will jump off you."

"Say, Huck," said Tom. "Will you let me go with you when you throw the cat?"

"Sure," said Huck. "I was planning on doing it tonight. Old Hoss Williams was buried last night and I reckon he was a very wicked man."

The two friends met in the graveyard later that night. The moon was almost full but the place looked spooky just the same. Tom and Huck hid under an elm tree to wait for the devils. They were scared and excited.

Soon they heard the sound of footsteps. Through a bush they saw a red glow floating among the graves.

"The devils are coming," shivered Tom.

"Don't be silly," whispered Huck. "That's a lantern. And the man carrying it is Muff Potter. That crook Injun Joe and Dr Robinson are with him. I don't trust Injun Joe, and why would a doctor be in his company?"

The three men stopped by Hoss William's grave. They'd brought shovels and a wheelbarrow with them. Muff and Injun Joe started digging.

"Hurry up," hissed Dr Robinson. "We don't want to be caught stealing corpses."

The other two continued digging until one of their spades hit something hard in the ground. Injun Joe jumped into the grave and Tom and Huck saw a coffin lid thrown out.

"He's looking mighty green," chuckled Muff, looking in the grave.

"Stop talking," snapped the doctor, "and bring him up."

Injun Joe climbed out of the grave. "Not unless you give us five more green ones."

"But I've already paid you," said Dr Robinson. "You agreed." He raised his fists to strike Injun Joe.

"Hey," said Muff, leaping out of the grave with a knife. "You leave Injun Joe alone."

Dr Robinson turned to face Muff. There was a fight at the edge of the grave. Muff slipped and fell, banging his head against the tombstone. The knife clattered to the ground and Muff lay unconscious.

Injun Joe snatched up the knife. "Remember the night you turned me away from your father's kitchen, doctor?" he snarled at Dr Robinson. "You said I was trying to burgle your house but I was only begging for bread. I swore then that I'd settle the score one day."

And he plunged Muff's knife in the doctor's chest. Just then the clouds blotted out the moon. Tom and Huck ran for their lives.

They didn't see Injun Joe placing the knife back in Muff's hand. And when Muff woke up, they didn't hear Injun Joe say, "Muff, you just murdered the doctor."

"We've got to keep quiet about this, Tom," gasped Huck when they had reached the safety of a ruined building on the edge of town. "If Injun Joe finds out we saw his crime, he'll be after us. I think we should swear a blood oath that we'll never talk to anyone about this."

"No one?" said Tom.

"Not as long as we draw breath," said Huck. He found a piece of slate and Tom wrote on it with chalk.

HUCK FINN AND TOM SAWYER SWEARS THEY WILL KEEP MUM ABOUT THIS AND THEY WISH THEY MAY DROP DOWN DEAD IN THEIR TRACKS IF THEY TELL AND ROT.

Then they both pricked their finger with a pin Tom had in his pocket and signed their names with blood. Huck buried the slate in the rubble, and the oath was complete.

When Tom finally climbed back through his bedroom window it was almost dawn. Sid was fast asleep. Tom spied a small parcel on the bed and his heart missed a beat. He unwrapped it slowly. Becky had thrown the doorknob through the window.

Running Away

The next morning, Muff was arrested. A gravedigger had discovered Dr Robinson's body. He'd also found Muff's knife, covered in blood.

"Huck," Tom said when they met after school, "Injun Joe lied. He swore he saw Muff do the murder. Muff might get hanged for Injun Joe's crime. And Injun Joe might go free."

"Yes, but he'll murder us if we talk," said Huck. "We're in grave danger. We can't break our oath."

There was nothing for it, thought Tom, but to run away to where there was no Injun Joe, and no Becky.

He missed school the next morning, and set off into the big wide world. He hadn't gone far, though, when he started to feel lost and lonely.

"Hello, Tom." Another boy was walking along the road, a large bundle bumping on his shoulder.

"Hello Joe Harper. Am I glad to see you."

"I wish you hadn't," said Joe. "I'm running away."

"Me too," said Tom. "No one loves me."

"Let's run away together," suggested Joe.

They decided to set up camp on Jackson's Island in the middle of the Mississippi River. No one lived there and it was full of trees. No one would find them.

"I'll tell Huck to come," said Tom. They found Huck swimming at his usual spot, and he gladly accepted to join them. He even had a raft which they used to cross the river to the island.

River Pirates

Once they were on the island, they built a fire to keep warm.

"We can be hermits and live on mouldy bread until we die of cold," said Joe.

"I say we should be river pirates," said Tom.

"What do pirates do?" asked Huck.

"Attack ships and steal treasures," answered Tom, "and they bury it in haunted places to be guarded by ghosts."

It all sounded great fun. But once night fell and they'd eaten all the food they'd brought with them, Tom started to miss his warm bed.

That feeling of homesickness was still there in the morning, but only a bit. The boys caught fish for breakfast, swam in the river and climbed trees.

In the afternoon, they heard a strange sound coming from the banks of the river opposite.

"Sounds like thunder," declared Tom.

"It can't be thunder," said Huck. "The sky's blue."

They rushed to the shore and peeped through the bushes. "Why," said Joe, "it's a ferryboat chugging by."

The ferryboat seemed to be drifting slowly with the current. Her decks were crowded with people. There were a lot of small rowing boats on the water too.

Then there was a loud boom, and a spout of water rose up in the air.

"They're looking for drowned people," said Huck. "I seen them doing that when Bill Turner fell in the river."

"How can firing cannons help find dead bodies?" asked Joe.

"The cannonball is supposed to make the dead bodies rise to the surface of the water," replied Huck.

"I wonder who drowned," said Tom.

"Don't you know?" laughed Huck. "It's us!"

"You mean they're looking for us? So soon?" gasped Tom. That made him feel better. Everyone was worried about them!

"We are loved after all," he declared. "Perhaps we should go back home."

The other two didn't agree. So when they had gone to sleep that night, Tom crossed the river on the raft.

Soon he was crouching underneath Aunt Polly's window. The light was still on in the parlour. Aunt Polly, Mary, Sid and Joe's mother were talking.

"I wish Tom was still alive," wailed Sid. "I'd never tell on him again. Still, if he'd led a better life..."

"Don't speak ill of my Tom," cried Aunt Polly. "He was a noble boy at heart, true to his friends and honest. And so were Joe and that poor motherless Huck. How am I going to get through the funeral on Sunday?"

At the mention of the funeral, Joe's mum and Mary started sobbing loudly. It made Tom want to cry too. He'd never known he was so noble and true.

Suddenly Tom had an idea. He'd show Joe and Huck just how much they were loved…

Back From the Dead

On Sunday morning, the church was full to bursting. Three coffins were laid out in front of the altar. They were empty, of course, since the bodies had not been found. Everyone was dressed in black, and crying.

Mr Sprague, the minister, spoke from the pulpit. He talked about how obedient Tom Sawyer had been to his aunt, and how kind to Mary and Sid.

He described how nobly Joe Harper had helped his mother with her chores. And how friendly and helpful Huckleberry Finn had been to everyone in town.

"They will be sorely missed," he said, "for never have three young men mattered so much to a town."

Suddenly a loud wailing arose from the door. Three boys in filthy clothes came in, crying their eyes out.

"Thank you, everyone," bawled the boy leading them. "It's nice to know you all think so highly of us."

It was Tom. He'd brought Joe and Huck to their own funerals.

Tom's friends began calling him a hero. "Why, Tom, you're as good as come back from the dead," said Ben.

Only Becky remained unfriendly.

"You are a rogue, Tom," she sniffed, "and a thorn in the side of your family."

Tom wished he could do something to change Becky's mind about him. And then, one afternoon, he got the chance...

Becky in Trouble

Mr Dobbins, the schoolteacher, kept a special book in his desk. It had a leather cover, and a ribbon for a bookmark. No one knew what he used it for, because no one was allowed to look in the teacher's desk.

One day during playtime, Becky took the book out. It was a doctor's manual, full of charts of skeletons.

Tom sneaked up behind her. "Becky, what are you doing?"

Becky jumped. The book fell out of her hands… and a page ripped.

"You're in big trouble now, Becky," said Tom. "I reckon that book is worth at least a million dollars."

At reading time, Mr Dobbins told the class to choose a book from the shelf. He reached into the desk for his book, and his eyes nearly jumped out of his head. "Who… has… torn… my… book?"

Everyone sat rigid with fright. "Not me, sir! Not me."

"Own up, whoever it is."

Tom heard Becky's chair scrape against the floor as she prepared to stand up. He leaped to his feet.

"I done it, sir."

Mr Dobbins's eyes fixed on Tom's like a cobra's.

"Come… here."

Tom knew what was coming. The cane! But he didn't care.

Becky smiled at him and whispered, "Tom, I love you."

Injun Joe Escapes

Muff Potter's trial in the courthouse for the murder of Dr Robinson started halfway through the summer holidays. Everyone was sure that he'd be hanged.

Micah from the store remembered selling Muff the knife used to kill Dr Robinson. Old Ma Grundy swore she'd seen him washing blood off his shirt in a stream.

Then Injun Joe came forward to be questioned in front of the judge. Tom and Huck, sitting with the rest of the town, squirmed with guilt. They knew the real story, and they knew Injun Joe was lying.

"Are you sure we can't rescue Muff?" Tom asked.

"Told you we can't," said Huck.

The trial continued day after day, with poor Muff sitting in the dock looking half dead already.

At last the moment came when the final witness was called forward. It was an old woman who had seen Muff sharpening his knife the day before the murder.

"I fear it'll be the gallows for the poor man," Tom heard Aunt Polly whisper to Joe Harper's mum.

Tom looked at Muff in the dock. He looked at Injun Joe scowling in his chair. And he jumped up.

"Injun Joe did it, Your Honour," he yelled. "I was in the graveyard and I seen it all…"

His words were interrupted by a loud crash. Injun Joe had leaped out of his seat and through the courthouse window. Everyone watched as he ran down the street, towards the woods…

The Haunted House

Tom was a hero again for saving Muff. But he dreaded going out alone. What if Injun Joe came looking for him under cover of darkness? He only relaxed when news came that the murderer had escaped over the border into Texas.

"Now that I've got my freedom back, we should celebrate by looking for treasure," said Tom to Huck.

"But where will we dig?" asked Huck.

"In a haunted house," replied Tom. "Robbers always bury treasure in haunted houses."

There was a big deserted house on a hill outside the town. Tom reckoned it was haunted, so they fetched a pick and a shovel and went to look it over. The place was a mess. The garden and the porch were choked with weeds. Most of the windows had fallen out of their frames. The floorboards were rotten.

"Let's have a look upstairs," said Huck. "I might find some shirts to wear." They went upstairs, leaving the pick and shovel in the hallway.

"Look, here's a trunk," said Tom.

But Huck poked him in the ribs. "Shh! Did you hear that? Someone's coming up the garden."

"Ghosts don't come in from outside," said Tom.

"It's not ghosts," whispered Huck. "I heard footsteps."

Both boys dodged away from the windows and stretched out on the floor. The floorboards under them were full of holes and through them they saw two men enter the ground floor. Tom recognized the first as the mysterious deaf Spaniard who'd turned up in town recently. He had an enormous bushy beard that hid half his face, and a big hat. The other man was very thin with long red hair.

"I don't like it here," the thin man said to the Spaniard. "It's spooky."

"Sissy!" replied the Spaniard. He spoke in a voice that both Tom and Huck recognized. It was Injun Joe! He'd never left town after all – he'd just put on a disguise.

"A bag of silver is good enough pay for a morning's thieving," said the thin man. "But why do we have to hide it here?"

"It'll only be for a few days till I get my revenge," said Injun Joe, "then we'll be going to Texas for real."

The word revenge made Tom go cold all over. Did that mean Injun Joe was coming for him? Huck nudged him. Injun Joe had taken a large bag of jingling coins out of his pocket. He lifted one of the paving stones in the fireplace and started digging up the earth underneath it with his knife.

Tom looked at Huck and winked, all fear instantly forgotten. Here was enough treasure to keep them in pies and cakes for a long time.

Suddenly Injun Joe stopped digging. "There's something else buried here," he said. "Help me dig it up. No wait, the wood is rotten. I've smashed the lid."

He pulled out his hand and it was full of gold coins. Treasure! Both men's eyes shone with delight.

"They did say a band of railway robbers used this house a few summers ago," said Injun Joe's friend. "What shall we do?"

"Dig it up," said Injun Joe. "Let's have a look at it."

"I saw a pick in the hallway," said his friend. "I'll fetch it."

He came back with Tom's pick, and started digging alongside Injun Joe. Soon they'd pulled a strongbox out of the hole, a real treasure chest. It was full to the brim with gold coins.

"It's a beauty," grinned Injun Joe, kissing the rotten box.

His friend did the same. "Where will we hide it?"

"I knows just the place for it," laughed Injun Joe. "Under the cross!"

"Under the cross," said Tom when Injun Joe and his friend had left. "Could that mean they're burying the gold in a grave?"

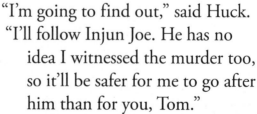

"I'm going to find out," said Huck. "I'll follow Injun Joe. He has no idea I witnessed the murder too, so it'll be safer for me to go after him than for you, Tom."

McDougal's Cave

Tom found Aunt Polly in a very good mood when he returned home. "I made you some pies and lemonade for the annual picnic tomorrow, Tom. I made Becky's favourite cake too."

The annual picnic was for youngsters and teachers only. A boat was hired and the lucky ones ferried three miles upriver to one of the nicest picnic spots in Missouri. The day was spent eating, swimming, playing games and exploring the famous McDougal's Cave.

"You going in the cave, Tom?" said Joe Harper.

"Me and Becky are both going," said Tom. "You're not afraid of the dark, are you, Joe?"

"It's not the dark you have to be afraid of," said Mr Dobbins as they gathered by the entrance, a slit in the rocks shaped like a giant A. "The cave is like a maze, and it's easy to get lost. Make sure you all have candles and matches, and don't wander off on your own. You will get lost if you do that."

Soon the cave was echoing to the sound of laughter as the children followed the guide through the dark. By the time they emerged to board the ferry, the sun was setting.

"Where's Tom?" Aunt Polly asked Joe Harper when the ferry returned to St Petersburg, where parents and relatives were clustered at the jetty.

"Where's Becky?" asked Mrs Thatcher.

Tom and Becky Get Lost

It seemed no one had seen Tom and Becky on the journey back home. No one remembered seeing them coming out of the caves either. They only remembered seeing them go in.

Aunt Polly went as white as a sheet. "They must have been left behind in McDougal's Cave," she wailed.

Inside the cave, Tom and Becky were trying not to panic.

"It's my fault we got lost," said Becky. "I insisted on finding out where those bats were hiding."

"I thought I knew the way back," replied Tom. "But we took a wrong turn somewhere. Let's shout. I'm sure we'll bump into the others."

They called out but no one answered. Tom insisted they keep walking. Soon they realized they were going round in circles. They heard the distant sound of the ferryboat's horn.

"They're leaving without us," cried Becky.

"They'll miss us and come looking for us, you'll see," said Tom.

They sat holding hands. Time passed.

"How long have we been here? It feels like days!"

"It's only been hours, Becky," said Tom. He pulled something out of his pocket. "Do you recognize this?"

"Yes, Tom," she answered as she felt the object he had in his hand. "It's a piece of the cake Aunt Polly made us. It's going to be our last…"

She didn't finish the sentence but Tom knew what she meant. Our last supper!

"Listen, Becky," he said. "We mustn't give up hope. They'll organize a search party and find us."

"Will they, Tom?"

"I am sure they will."

Becky ate the last piece of cake. She drifted off to sleep, and Tom closed his eyes. Perhaps if he went to sleep too, he'd have a wonderful dream. He had no idea how long he lay there but gradually he became aware of a sound. Footsteps! Tom was about to wake up Becky, when the light of a candle came round the corner.

"Hello?" he called.

The light stopped moving and, in a flash, Tom saw who was carrying it. Injun Joe! The thief gasped, turned and fled. Tom reckoned he couldn't have recognized him in the dark or else he'd have attacked.

"Have they found us," said Becky.

"Ssh," said Tom. "It was only a bat. Go back to sleep." He couldn't tell Becky how terrified he was. They mustn't run into Injun Joe again.

"Listen Becky, we need to move. Perhaps we'll stumble across the entrance." They started walking. They had no idea how long they wandered but at last they heard faint voices.

"Hello, Tom? Becky?" Tom recognized one of them. Joe Harper's dad.

"We're here," he called. "We're here…"

"Let's Go Find the Treasure."

Tom opened his eyes. He was tucked up in bed. Aunt Polly was clutching his hand.

"How long have I been lying here, Aunt Polly?"

"Nearly a week. Oh, Tom, you were lost for three days, like Jonah in the belly of the fish. You were lucky to come out of them caves with just a fever. People have been known to starve to death in there."

"Not that anyone is likely to explore those caves again. Judge Thatcher had the entrance sealed with a wooden door," added Mary who'd been sitting with Aunt Polly.

"Sealed?" cried Tom. "But Injun Joe is in there."

"Hush, now," said Aunt Polly. "You're too weak to fret. Lie back."

Tom felt dizzy again. Mary put a damp towel on his forehead and he went to sleep again. When he woke up, Huck was sitting in the room.

"Injun Joe's no more, Tom," he said. "Aunt Polly gave a message to Judge Thatcher who sent some armed men to go back to McDougal's Cave. They found him dead behind the door. The man died of sheer terror."

"I reckon he hid the treasure in those caves," said Tom. "He must have been worried about it when he heard about the picnic and went in there to make sure it was safe. The entrance to the cave is barred now, Huck, but I reckon we could find our way in somehow."

"Let's go find the treasure, then," said Huck.

"Find what?" asked Aunt Polly who'd come into the room with some beef broth for Tom. "Tom ain't going anywhere. It'll take at least a week till he can walk."

Tom sneaked out through the window the very next morning, taking a sack of tools with him. He and Huck met on the edge of town and went down river on a raft.

"How are we going to get in, Tom?" asked Huck.

"I saw a hole in the roof when Becky and I were wandering around," said Tom. "We couldn't reach it. But I reckon we can lower ourselves down from the outside. We just have to find it."

They found the hole in the ground above the cave, hidden behind the branches of a prickly bush. Tom tied one end of a rope to a nearby tree trunk and let it down through the hole. They then lowered themselves down the rope till they were standing on solid ground. Huck fished out a ball of kite string from the sack and tied the end to the rope.

"I'll unwind the string as we go along and it'll guide us back to the hole," he explained.

They lit a lantern and wandered around in the dark.

"Where do you reckon Injun Joe hid the gold, Tom?" asked Huck.

"We gotta look," said Tom.

But hours later they had found nothing. They were about to give up, when they came across a trail of footprints.

Tom's a Hero

"They look like they were made by Injun Joe's boots," gasped Huck. They followed the trail. It led them to a rock at the far end of a tunnel.

"Do you see that, Huck," cried Tom, holding up the lantern. "There's a cross painted on this rock."

"It's the cross Injun Joe mentioned in the haunted house," said Tom. "This must be it, Huck."

Huck was looking at the ground. "The earth here has been disturbed."

They scooped the dirt away with their bare hands, revealing wooden boards. Under them was a black hole, the entrance to a secret passage.

"Come on, Tom," said Huck. They crawled down on their bellies, worming their way along the passage. It opened into a little cave and there was the strongbox.

Huck opened it. "The gold's all here, Tom. We're rich, I tell you! We can buy all the ice cream in Missouri and Texas combined…"

Later, Aunt Polly was standing by Tom's empty bed, shaking her head. "That boy will be the death of me yet."

"Tom's a hero, Mama," said Mary.

"He'll be your ruin, Aunt Polly," said Sid.

"Will I?" A grimy face appeared at the bedroom window, followed by another. It was Tom and Huck.

"We've got a present for you, Aunt Polly," said Tom, and a moment later he and Huck poured a pile of gold on to the bed.

About the author

Mark Twain's real name was Samuel L Clemens. He was born in Missouri, USA in 1835. As a young man he was a pilot, steering large boats and barges on the Mississippi River. He later became a journalist and writer. He took his pen name from the riverboatman's cry "Mark Twain", meaning 'mark number two', which implied that the water was deep enough for a boat to float. He travelled widely in the United States, and to Europe. He wrote many stories and accounts of his travels, but it was memories of his childhood growing up on the banks of the Mississippi River that were the basis of his greatest books, *The Adventures of Tom Sawyer* published in 1876, and its sequel, *The Adventures of Huckleberry Finn*. He died in 1907 aged 74.

Other titles in the Classic Collection series:

*Alice's Adventures in Wonderland • Little Women
The Three Musketeers • Treasure Island • Pinocchio
20,000 Leagues Under the Sea • Heidi • The Wizard of Oz
Gulliver's Travels • Robinson Crusoe • Robin Hood • Black Beauty
The Secret Garden • Anne of Green Gables • The Little Princess*

A NEW BURLINGTON BOOK
The Old Brewery
6 Blundell Street
London N7 9BH

QED Project Editor: Alexandra Koken
Managing Editor: Victoria Garrard • Design Manager: Anna Libecka
Editor: Maurice Lyon • Designer: Rachel Clark
Copyright © QED Publishing 2013

First published in the UK in 2013 by
QED Publishing, A Quarto Group company,
230 City Road, London EC1V 2TT

www.qed-publishing.co.uk

A catalogue record for this book is available from the British Library.

ISBN 978 1 78171 353 2

Printed in China